A Note to Parents and Caregivers:

Read-it! Readers are for children who are just starting on the amazing road to reading. These beautiful books support both the acquisition of reading skills and the love of books.

 The PURPLE LEVEL presents basic topics and objects using high frequency words and simple language patterns.

 The RED LEVEL presents familiar topics using common words and repeating sentence patterns.

 The BLUE LEVEL presents new ideas using a larger vocabulary and varied sentence structure.

 The YELLOW LEVEL presents more challenging ideas, a broad vocabulary, and wide variety in sentence structure.

 The GREEN LEVEL presents more complex ideas, an extended vocabulary range, and expanded language structures.

 The ORANGE LEVEL presents a wide range of ideas and concepts using challenging vocabulary and complex language structures.

When sharing a book with your child, read in short stretches, pausing often to talk about the pictures. Have your child turn the pages and point to the pictures and familiar words. And be sure to reread favorite stories or parts of stories.

There is no right or wrong way to share books with children. Find time to read with your child, and pass on the legacy of literacy.

Adria F. Klein, Ph.D.
Professor Emeritus
California State University
San Bernardino, California

To Emile ... and his funny father

First American edition published in 2005 by
Picture Window Books
5115 Excelsior Boulevard
Suite 232
Minneapolis, MN 55416
877-845-8392
www.picturewindowbooks.com

First published in Canada in 2000 by
Les éditions Héritage inc.
300 Arran Street, Saint Lambert
Quebec, Canada J4R 1K5

Printed in the United States of America.

Library of Congress Cataloging-in-Publication Data
Villeneuve, Mireille.
Felicio's incredible invention / Mireille Villeneuve ; [illustrated by] Anne Villeneuve.
p. cm. — (Read-it! readers)
Summary: Felicio, a young inventor, attempts to create the perfect present for his father's birthday, hoping that it will make his very serious father laugh.
ISBN 1-4048-1030-7 (hardcover)
[1. Inventions—Fiction. 2. Fathers and sons—Fiction. 3. Birthdays—Fiction.
4. Laughter—Fiction.] I. Villeneuve, Anne, ill. II. Title. III. Series.

PZ7.V73Fe 2004
[E]—dc22
2004023775

Felicio's Incredible Invention

By Mireille Villeneuve
Illustrated by Anne Villeneuve

Special thanks to our advisers for their expertise:

Adria F. Klein, Ph.D.
Professor Emeritus, California State University
San Bernardino, California

Susan Kesselring, M.A.
Literacy Educator
Rosemount - Apple Valley - Eagan (Minnesota) School District

PICTURE WINDOW BOOKS
Minneapolis, Minnesota

Mr. Bartholemy was always very serious—even when he was wearing his striped pajamas.

Every morning, he put on his best suit to go to work. Then he swallowed a quick breakfast.

Gulp! Down the hatch!

Felicio spied on his father through his binoculars. He wrote everything down in a little notebook.

When he eats his cereal, my father looks very serious.

Felicio designed a costume to make his father laugh. With a funny wig and false nose, Felicio became the fabulous Popov the Clown.

He took out his trumpet and played a great DO-DO-DO-DO-DOOO-DOOO! Then he turned cartwheels, and confetti rained down.

At the end of his act, Popov the Clown landed in front of his father and said, "Howdee doodee to you, Mr. Bartholemy! Nice day for planting radishes, wouldn't you say?"

Mr. Bartholemy looked at his son, as sad as a dog that's lost its bone.

Felicio wrote, *Even when entertained by Popov the Clown, my father looks serious.*

The boy sighed. Soon it would be his father's birthday. To celebrate it, Felicio wanted to make his father laugh. But could he succeed?

Ding! Felicio got an idea. The young inventor locked himself up in his laboratory. He sketched out his plans and made a lot of noise in the process.

After a long day's work, Mr. Bartholemy returned home.

12

Felicio opened the door to his laboratory.
He carried a strange-looking armchair into
the living room, then asked his father to
sit down on it. Mr. Bartholemy did as he
was told.

All of a sudden, the chair's arms grew very
long! They started tickling Mr. Bartholemy
all over.

Felicio's father jumped into the air. Then he fell onto the floor. BANG! BOOM! CRASH!

"Oof! This armchair isn't comfortable at all," Mr. Bartholemy complained.

Felicio wrote, *When someone tickles him, my father gets hurt.*

Mr. Bartholemy went and lay down on the sofa.

Felicio produced his next invention: a hippopotamus mouth that told jokes and clattered its teeth when it laughed. In the middle of the best joke, Mr. Bartholemy started snoring.

Felicio noted, *When you tell him jokes, my father falls asleep.*

But Felicio wasn't discouraged. He came up with another idea, a chocolate-covered one this time.

With his grandmother's help, he made a trick cake. When you cut it, the cake would explode into a thousand pieces.

Once they finished making the cake, Grandma Bartholemy exclaimed, "Oh no, I forgot. Your father never eats dessert!"

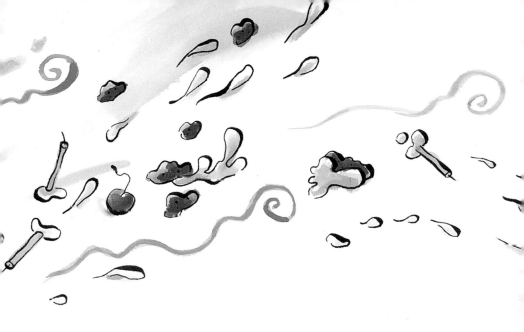

Felicio was very sad. He gave the cake to the neighbor's dog. KA-BOOM!

For his birthday, I'll just have to give him a tie, Felicio wrote, with tears in his eyes.

That evening, before he went to bed, Felicio asked his grandmother, "Why doesn't Papa ever laugh?"

"Your father is very tired," she answered.

"Why is he so tired?" Felicio asked.

"Because he's very busy," she said.

In his notebook, Felicio wrote, *My father
always has a good reason for everything.*

Then he turned off the light and tried
to fall asleep.

Suddenly, a little tune slipped into his ears.
It was coming from the bathroom.

Very quietly, Felicio crept toward the shower.
And what did he see? A very happy man
singing. Felicio pinched himself and rubbed
his eyes.

No, he wasn't dreaming ...
that really was his father!

After his shower, Mr. Bartholemy became very
serious again. But Felicio knew what to do.
He knew the present his father needed.

The next day, Felicio went back into his
laboratory. What was he building?
Who could tell?

He hung a sign on the door:
Do not disturb!

Finally, it was Mr. Bartholemy's birthday.

WHOOSH! Felicio dove onto his father's bed.
"Happy birthday, Papa!"

His father opened his eyes. He saw something
that wasn't very serious at all: Felicio's present!

29

Mr. Bartholemy has a new job now.
Instead of putting on his best suit,
he puts on his shower to go to work.

Where he works, people call him
Rigoletto. He's the clown who sings
in the shower.

In his new notebook, Felicio wrote,
Even at work, my father is never serious!

More *Read-it!* Readers

Bright pictures and fun stories help you practice your reading skills. Look for more books at your level.

Alex and the Team Jersey by Gilles Tibo
Alex and Toolie by Gilles Tibo
Clever Cat by Karen Wallace
Daddy's a Busy Beaver by Bruno St-Aubin
Daddy's a Dinosaur by Bruno St-Aubin
Felicio's Incredible Invention by Mireille Villeneuve
Flora McQuack by Penny Dolan
Izzie's Idea by Jillian Powell
Mysteries for Felicio by Mireille Villeneuve
Naughty Nancy by Anne Cassidy
Parents Do the Weirdest Things! by Louise Tondreau-Levert
Peppy, Patch, and the Postman by Marisol Sarrazin
Peppy, Patch, and the Socks by Marisol Sarrazin
The Princess and the Frog by Margaret Nash
The Roly-Poly Rice Ball by Penny Dolan
Run! by Sue Ferraby
Sausages! by Anne Adeney
Stickers, Shells, and Snow Globes by Dana Meachen Rau
Theodore the Millipede by Carole Tremblay
The Truth About Hansel and Gretel by Karina Law
Willie the Whale by Joy Oades

Looking for a specific title or level? A complete list of *Read-it!* Readers is available on our Web site: *www.picturewindowbooks.com*